BREAKDOWN

THE ATLAS OF CURSED PLACES

BREAKDOWN

KATHRYN J. BEHERNS

darby creek

MINNEAPOLIS

Darby Creek
A division of Lerner Publishing Group, Inc.
241 First Avenue North
Minneapolis, MN 55401 USA

For reading levels and more information, look up this title at www.lernerbooks.com.

The image in this book is used with the permission of: © Andreiuc88/Dreamstime.com (man in cave); © Andreiuc88/Dreamstime.com (man on rock); © iStockphoto.com/ mustafahacalaki (skull); © iStockphoto.com/Igor Zhuravlov (storm); © iStockphoto. com/desifoto (graph paper); © iStockphoto.com/Trifonenko (blue flame); © iStockphoto.com/Anita Stizzoli (dark clouds).

Main body text set in Janson Text LT Std 12/17.5.
Typeface provided by Adobe Systems.

Library of Congress Cataloging-in-Publication Data

The Cataloging-in-Publication Data for *Breakdown* is on file at the Library of Congress.
ISBN 978-1-5124-1323-6 (lib. bdg.)
ISBN 978-1-5124-1347-2 (pbk.)
ISBN 978-1-5124-1348-9 (EB pdf)

Manufactured in the United States of America
1-39782-21320-4/7/2016

To all of my former students

CHAPTER 1

Owen wrapped his arms around Maddy's waist. She felt his warm breath on her ear.

"Have I met you before?" Owen asked as a joke.

"Better be careful," Maddy replied, grinning at the silliness. "I have a boyfriend and he is big and strong and will be here any minute."

He looked really good with his perfectly messy hair and blue shirt that matched his clear blue eyes. She stood on her tiptoes and gave him a kiss. Owen and Maddy had been dating since ninth grade.

"I know I say this all the time, but really, you look amazing," said Owen.

The restaurant was built into the side of the riverbank. It used to be a cave. Now it had high, arched ceilings with crystal chandeliers twinkling. They followed the waiter across the long dining room and around couples quietly talking. As Maddy got closer to their table in the back of the restaurant, she noticed a large bouquet of daisies there. Owen pulled Maddy's chair out for her.

Owen said with a huge grin on his face, "You mean so much to me, Maddy. We're seniors. Only one more year together. I don't want to take it for granted."

"We're going to college. We're not dying. You can't get rid of me that easily." She winked at him. "Daisies, my favorite." She reached out to grab a daisy. Instead she bumped her drink.

It spilled all over the table, dribbling down the little black dress that she had borrowed from her mom.

"Leave it to me to ruin a romantic moment," said Maddy.

"If you didn't do something clumsy, then I definitely would have. That's how I roll."

Maddy grinned as she stood up.

The bathrooms were in a hallway on the side of the main room. Just inside the ladies' room was a woman with short red hair and a gray dress—almost the same color as her skin.

"You waiting?" Maddy asked the woman. There was something about her that seemed very old, yet she looked just a little older than Maddy.

"You could say that," replied the woman with the pale face.

"So," Maddy said, trying to make conversation, "you come here often?"

The woman burst out in an awkward laugh. "I'm here all the time," she said. She looked Maddy in the eyes. Blood started to drip from the woman's left nostril.

"Oh, God! Your nose is bleeding," said Maddy.

With absolutely no expression, she wiped her nose with her gray—almost blue—hand.

Then, as though she hadn't talked to anyone in years, she started to babble. "There was this horrible massacre that happened seventy-six years ago. A woman stormed in here and started killing people. The woman was possessed by evil, and she couldn't stop herself." Her words came out fast and desperate, more like a confession than a story.

"You wouldn't believe the blood. It was splattered right here on this wall. A young couple held each other on that bench there. The young man ran in here when he heard his girlfriend screaming. Their eyes—oh God, their eyes. She killed them, too. She didn't want to, but her body wasn't under her control anymore."

The pain in the woman's eyes was so real. It was as though she had been there on the night she was describing. But that was impossible. This woman was only in her twenties.

Clearly, she had lost her mind. She stared into Maddy's dark brown eyes. "Have you ever had your mind scream, but your body do nothing?"

Maddy knew what the woman was talking about. She remembered back to when she was a little girl. She used to watch her dad beat her mom. As a little girl she would hide in the coat closet and peek through the crack in the door. She wanted to scream at him him, to stop him, to save her mom, but all she could do was hide until it was over. Then when he had passed out, she would curl up beside her mom.

The woman was now staring off into space. Lips quivering, she said, "There is evil. Evil that can take over someone's body. Even if their mind screams NO! The evil can still take your body. And all you can do is scream inside your mind." Then she grabbed Maddy by the wrist and whispered as if someone might hear, "It was Pike."

Her hand was as cold as ice. Maddy yelped and ripped her arm free.

A look of terror came over the woman's face. She shouted, "It is P—!"

Before she could finish the statement there was a loud rumble. A brick fell from the ceiling. Then the ceiling collapsed altogether—right on top of the woman. The only thing that could be seen under the rubble was one corner of the bench she had been sitting on. Maddy screamed, "Help! Please, somebody help!" Maddy clawed helplessly at the heavy pile of bricks and old mortar.

CHAPTER 2

Screams from the main room could be heard. The power was out, and because the restaurant was built into the riverbank, there were no windows. The whole place was in darkness. Cell phones became flashlights.

"It's caving in! Run! We're going to be trapped!" someone shouted.

Everyone in the restaurant dashed to the exit. Owen shouted for Maddy as the crowd of people pushed him toward the door. Owen scooped up a thin, elderly man who had tripped in all the panic. People were stepping on each other. Owen rescued others who had fallen in the frenzy to the exit, one person after another. The restaurant was almost empty. Still no Maddy. Outside Owen looked through the crowd, thinking she must have made it out already. But she was nowhere to be found. He tried to go back in, but people stopped him. It was too dangerous, they said.

"But Madison Connelly is in there. My Maddy is in there!" he shouted desperately.

He ran over to the side door used by employees only. Once inside, he turned on his cell phone light. In the blue beam he could see Maddy on her hands and knees drenched in sweat and dirt. She was scraping at a pile of rubble. He tried not to look at her fingers. They were bloody and sliced up from the digging.

"Maddy! We have to get out of here," Owen said. "This whole place could collapse any second."

"I can't! She was right here, sitting. She told me about a massacre and Pike. I have to find her. I won't leave her behind."

"We have to go, Maddy." Owen pulled Maddy up by her waist.

"She was sitting right there!" Maddy pointed to the pile that was as high as the ceiling. "She's under here."

Owen knew how determined Maddy could be, so he bent low to her ear. "Maddy, you're not strong enough, babe. There are rescue people coming who know how to find people. We'll make sure they search here first. They have the strength and equipment to get her out *safely*. Now, please, Maddy, trust me."

Maddy knew he was right, but he still had to drag her away.

The wait felt like hours. Finally firefighters arrived and Maddy told them about the woman. They searched for her amid the rubble, and then spoke again with Maddy.

"We didn't find anyone. We lifted the rubble, even dug up the pile of sandstone. Nothing. She may have been there right before the collapse, but she was not there during the collapse."

Maddy couldn't believe it. "You're wrong! She was sitting there on the bench."

"We found the bench. Nothing else."

"I watched the ceiling fall on top of her," pleaded Maddy.

"Unless she disappeared into thin air, there is no way a woman was sitting where you say."

Maddy tried to run toward the restaurant. A firefighter restrained her, wrapped his arms around her. "Listen! Our minds can play tricks on us, especially when something bad happens."

"But I—" Maddy started to cry.

"I know you think you saw someone, but we can't always trust what we see," the firefighter said.

A familiar voice shouted from a squad car, "Come on, Maddy! I'll give you a ride home!" It was Sergeant Riley, one of her mom's coworkers. The firefighter and Owen walked Maddy to the police car.

Owen leaned in and gave her a kiss goodbye. Maddy could still see the woman's icy blue eyes. She remembered the woman's last words: "It is Pike." The very name, Pike, felt wrong, like a curse.

The squad car slowly pulled away. "You okay, kiddo?" Sergeant Riley had known Maddy since she was eight.

"Yeah, I'm thinking about what happened," replied Maddy.

"In all my years on the force, I've come to realize there are some things we just can't explain. Take the latest case your mom is trying to solve. A couple, man and woman, missing. Their car must have broken down during that severe thunderstorm last week. We found their hiking gear. We even found their shoes, but no couple. The only clue is the word 'Pike' etched into the rearview mirror."

Goosebumps raced up Maddy's back. "Who is Pike?" she asked.

"Or *what* is pike? I have no idea. That's why your mom gets paid the big bucks. She's the best." Sergeant Riley went on, "And to think, when I first met her, you guys were living in a shelter, hiding from some jerk."

"Pretty crazy," Maddy agreed. They pulled up in front of a small green house with white shutters.

Sergeant Riley slowly pulled over. "Say hi to your mom for me."

Maddy waved as she walked up to the door. In the light from her house, Maddy could see marks on her forearm from the woman in the restaurant. She was real.

CHAPTER 3

Mom was waiting at the kitchen table like she always did when Maddy was out late. She'd been listening to the police scanner all evening so she knew exactly what had happened at the restaurant.

Maddy saw the two creases between her mom's eyebrows. "You were really worried, huh?" Maddy asked.

"Madison Fiona Connelly! Of course I was. I'm supposed to do that." And then she grabbed Maddy and squeezed her tight. "I don't know what I would do without my Mouse."

She was the only one who called Maddy that nickname. When Maddy was born, she was so tiny that her mom called her "Mouse." The name stuck.

"It was really crazy, Mom. I talked to this woman. She told me about a massacre that happened at the restaurant. She said, 'It was Pike.' And then in the middle of her sentence, the ceiling collapsed on top of her."

Maddy's mom shifted nervously in her chair. Her worry wrinkles returned. "Did you say Pike?"

"Yeah. Sergeant Riley told me about that breakdown case and what was etched in the rearview mirror."

Mom was angry. "He told you about that? That man has got a big mouth." Mom liked to keep Maddy totally out of the cases she was trying to solve. She said it wasn't for kids. "Let me see these." Mom reached over and grabbed Maddy's hands.

The fingernails were ripped and torn away. Her knuckles had deep gouges like she had been fighting a brick wall and had lost. Even the palms of her hands had scratches and cuts across them.

"Maddy, what were you thinking?" Her mom was more concerned than angry.

"There was a woman sitting there. I swear. I saw her. She grabbed me, Mom." Maddy shoved her bruised arm in front of her mom.

"I believe that someone grabbed you. But it would have to take one heck of a strong woman to make that kind of a bruise." Mom's cheeks were red. She clenched her teeth while she spoke. "Are you sure you and Owen are okay? I mean, you can be honest with me."

Maddy's mom did not trust men. Even though Owen was one of the kindest people Maddy knew, her mom did not like him. No man would ever be good enough for her little Mouse.

"Mom! Owen would *never* do something like this! He is the one who got me out of there." Maddy was hurt that her mom would accuse Owen of abuse, but she also understood where her mom came from. It was just over ten years ago when Maddy's mom packed them up and ran from Maddy's father.

"Looking at those bloody hands, I'm surprised you didn't have to haul Owen out. I have never met a guy so afraid of blood."

Mom gently washed the sand out of Maddy's ripped-up fingers and hands. She put a lavender-scented salve on them and then wrapped them in gauze.

"So do you believe me—that someone was there?" Maddy asked.

Mom's eyes got real small, like she was about to say something very important. "Maddy, there have been some really strange things happening in this city. If you tell me that you were talking with a ghost, I believe you," she said. "I've got to go to bed. I'm getting up early."

"You're working? But it's Sunday."

"I'll be working every day until this case is solved." Mom stopped. Maddy could see she was thinking. "You sure the woman said Pike?"

"Yeah, Mom, Pike. It was one of her last words to me."

Mom's worry wrinkles came back. "Good night."

"Good night, Mom."

Early that morning, while it was still dark, Maddy's mom entered her room. She grabbed Maddy's face and gave her a firm kiss on the cheek. "I love you, little Mouse."

Her hand was trembling. The last time Maddy saw her mom shaking was when they had to move into the women's shelter to hide from her father. Maddy never saw him again. Mom said that was a good thing. After that night, her mom went back to school for Criminal Justice. She'd pretty much been fearless ever since. So when her mom trembled, a red flag went up in Maddy's mind. There was something wrong.

"You okay?" Maddy mumbled, rubbing her eyes.

"Yeah, I'm just going to be away a lot," said her mom.

"Don't forget the peanut butter and jelly." They lived off of peanut butter and jelly. Her mom often forgot to eat when she was working on a case.

Mom smiled and patted her work bag. "Got 'em."

From the hallway there was enough light to see a large red leather book sticking out of her mom's bag. It was about four inches thick, worn on the corners, with what looked like gold letters inscribed across the binding.

"Geez, Mom. Doing a little heavy reading, are you?" said Maddy.

Mom got all awkward. "Oh, it's nothing. Just something for the case." Then she gave Maddy a long hug and said quietly, again, "I love you. See you soon, Mouse."

"Love you too, Mom."

Mom glanced back from the doorway. Her eyes looked sad.

CHAPTER 4

Her mother screamed. Pounded on the window glass. *Maddy!* she yelled. She was trapped in her squad car like a giant bubble sinking. Maddy could only watch as her mother was buried under the green-brown water of the Mississippi River. Her mom was still screaming, but by now Maddy could barely make out the words. She strained her eyes, trying to make out the words through the windshield: "It is Pike." Like a light switch, Mom's eyes changed from looking at her to a wide-eyed all-encompassing death stare.

Maddy woke up in hysteria, screaming and crying. She was drenched in sweat. The bandages on her hands were pulled off. The dream had felt so real. Her body ached from the night before, and now her mind reeled. She couldn't get away from this name, Pike. He seemed to be everywhere.

She glanced at the clock. It was 11:22 a.m. She sent a text to her mom. "Just checking in. Hope ur okay." She went to the kitchen table and poured a bowl of cereal. The house felt so empty. There was an eerie stillness, like the calm right before a tornado. Maddy picked up her phone. No text from her mom yet. She called Owen.

"Hey, babe! How are you?" asked Owen.

"Okay." Maddy couldn't shake this feeling that something was wrong. "Just wondering if you want to come over."

"Sure. I have to finish up some chores. Then I'll be there."

Owen showed up with donuts and a peppermint mocha—her favorite. Maddy grabbed him and hugged him as though her life depended on it.

"I have this crazy feeling like there is something wrong. I keep hearing this name, Pike. The last words of the woman in the restaurant were 'It is Pike.' This missing couple in a case my mom is working on also had the word *Pike* etched into the rearview mirror of their broken-down car. Even in my dream the name Pike came up."

She knew she could tell Owen anything, even if it sounded crazy. He had a way of making sense of things.

"Slow down, Maddy. Take a deep breath." Owen was holding her close. "Who is Pike?"

"I don't know. I just think he is someone very bad," replied Maddy. "And my mom is in trouble."

"Why are you whispering?"

"I don't know. It just feels like his name should be whispered."

"So where does your mom come in?" asked Owen.

"I just had this dream where I watched my mom drown. Her last words were 'It is Pike.' It might mean nothing, but what if . . . ?"

"What?"

"This dream was different. Like it wasn't a dream at all but a message."

Maddy was the most no-drama kind of person Owen knew. If she was saying that this stuff happened, then chances are it really did. Even if there was almost no proof.

"So what's our next move?" He would do anything for Madison Fiona Connelly, even if it meant hunting down ghosts.

Maddy replied, "I think we should check her desk here at home. Maybe it can tell us where she is or at least where she's heading."

CHAPTER 5

Maddy pushed the door to her mom's office open very slowly and quietly. This room was forbidden. She knew she would be in big trouble if her mom found out, and she always found out. The sun shone into the office. On the wall hung diplomas and degrees. There was a large desk that took up much of the room. On that desk were pictures of Maddy as a little girl and even during the awkward middle school years. She had a colorful lump of clay that Maddy made when she was seven. And between all of these mementos and memories were stacks and stacks of papers. Her mom was messy, but when asked to find something among these papers, she knew exactly where to look.

Maddy silently opened one of the desk drawers. She carefully pulled out a stack of tan and blue files. Even though she knew her mom wasn't home, Maddy somehow felt that at any moment, her mom would come bursting through the door and yell at her to mind her own business. Maddy handed the stack to Owen to look through. The files were filled with old receipts and pictures of past crime scenes.

Owen's mind raced. Pictures of chalk outlines of dead bodies. He could feel his hands shake. Splatters of blood on white walls. His knees quivered as he looked at cream-colored carpet drenched in victims' blood. That was it. Owen collapsed onto the ground. All his life he had this reaction to blood. He went down like a dead man.

"Oh, crap!" Maddy ran to him. She was used to seeing blood and hearing about gore. It was part of being her mom's daughter. Still, some people just didn't have the stomach for it. Maddy had forgotten Owen was one of those people.

After a few seconds he started to wake up.

"Hey, sleepyhead." Maddy combed his hair with her fingers. "I'm sorry. I should have been more sensitive."

"No, I should stop being such a wuss," replied Owen. He slowly sat up.

"I think it's kind of cute." Maddy leaned in and kissed him. "Every superman has his kryptonite."

Owen gently touched her cheek. "I love you, Maddy." He gave her a long kiss. Then there was a long silence. They both felt uncomfortable.

Owen broke the silence. "You don't have to say it back or anything. I just want you to know that." Owen was blushing now. He felt so stupid.

"I know I don't. I'm just thinking. I want to make sure I really mean it when I say it to you. I mean, it's a really big deal. I have never loved *any* man."

Owen smiled and slowly stood up. "No, I get it. At least you like me," he said, grinning. "Which is more than I can say for your mom."

They turned their attention back to the desk. To their surprise, there was a sticky note right in the middle of the desk. Had it been there the whole time? Why hadn't they noticed it? On the sticky note was an address: 999 Black Swamp Road, Lilydale, MN. It was underlined three times.

"What do you think?" asked Maddy.

"Let's go!"

CHAPTER 6

Owen slammed on his brakes. "Is that it?"

"No. That's the same road we just went down," said Maddy, trying to hide her frustration.

They had been driving back and forth for about twenty minutes. Everything looked the same. Same huge trees lining the road. Same faded and peeling billboards. Even the intersections looked the same with their wooden street signs and old street lamps.

Until, finally, they spotted an unmarked gravel road. It was so narrow, Owen had driven right past it.

"We haven't tried that one yet." He backed up to turn onto the road.

Large, bare trees arched over the entrance. Their branches clawed the roof of Owen's car, making screeching noises. It was like the trees didn't want anyone to enter. The road curved sharply to the left and then turned into a steep hill. They drove down into what looked like a dried-up swamp. At the bottom was a faded wooden street sign: Black Swamp Road. There was a cluster of worn-out houses with boarded windows and broken stoops. Many had dogs on chains, barking. Owen drove around the road that encircled the very small, unkempt community.

"That house is 993 and that one is 1001," he said. "The house between those two should be 999 but instead it is 666. That's an omen I don't appreciate."

"That has to be the house," Maddy said.

It was small, with a rusted metal roof. It had a porch with a broken swing. They followed the cracked and broken sidewalk.

As they stepped, Maddy noticed something slithering in the brown grass.

"Did you see that?" Another rustle of grass. "A snake!"

She grabbed Owen and wrapped herself around him. "You're afraid of snakes? How did I not know that?"

He ran with Maddy up to the porch. By the time they reached the house, he noticed many snakes darting around in the grass. He didn't say anything. He didn't want to scare Maddy even more.

"The house is actually 999 like on my mom's sticky note. The numbers just came loose and flipped upside-down. No omen. See?"

Maddy stepped up to the dilapidated porch and rang the doorbell. Waited. Rang again. More waiting. And again. This time they heard footsteps and some yelling. Then silence. Maddy pounded on the door. Finally, they heard three different locks turn, two chains sliding back, and a click. The door opened a crack. An old man poked his red nose out.

He shouted in a gravelly voice, "We don't want no popcorn, pizzas, cookies, or magazines, ya hear? We ain't buyin' what you're selling!"

He was about to slam the door but Maddy stuck her foot in it. The man looked at her with contempt. His lip curled. He swore under his breath. He was so angry he could hardly get the words out. "Move that foot before I make you move it, little lady. Ain't your mama teach you manners?"

"I'm sorry, sir. That's why we're here. We're looking for my mom. I think she might have come this way."

"Nobody come this way except by mistake."

He was about to shut the door on them when a high-pitched voice hollered from a distance.

"Yeah, we seen her!" The lady sounded like she was holding her nose, except she wasn't. "Let those kids in. Girl has worry in her voice."

"And she should if she knows what's best," said the old man. "Come in." He opened the door just enough to let them in.

Their house was tiny. The windows—the ones that weren't boarded up—were covered in a thick layer of dirt. There was a strong odor of cat pee and mothballs. The woman led them into a sitting room where a fluorescent light flickered from above. She was a big woman with huge arms and a thick waist. She wore an old apron that looked like it was once pretty. She looked like *she* was once pretty.

"Name's LouAnn," she said.

"I'm Maddy and this is my friend Owen."

Owen looked at Maddy and raised an eyebrow, as if to say, "I am a little more than a friend."

Maddy winked at him.

As they sat on a lumpy couch, they were surrounded by eyes. There were twenty—maybe more—dead, stuffed animals staring at them. They looked so real. They once were real, but each one of these animals had been killed, skinned, and stuffed with plastic to look like it was still alive. There were squirrels permanently paused in the middle of gathering acorns, a fawn forever folded up in its napping position. There were muskrats and beavers gnawing on shiny, varnished tree chunks. Scattered among all the dead animals were little stuffed mice frozen in mid-scurry.

"We used to own a taxidermy. Merl here is a real artist, isn't he?" She motioned to all the alive-looking animals that were *very* dead.

"Yeah," replied Owen. "He, ah, sure did a great job."

"He still does," LouAnn said. "He still stuffs animals. You got a dog or a cat you just can't go without? Merl here can make it look so real you'll want it to curl up at the foot of your bed."

Merl looked bashful. "I sure can. Them are my favorite projects."

"Can you stuff a human?" Owen said just loud enough for Maddy to hear.

She burst out laughing, then tried to gracefully switch subjects. "Sooooo . . . My mom. She is a detective for the St. Paul Police Department. Her name is Eleanor Connelly. She may have passed through here."

LouAnn interjected, "She sure did. That's why I invited you in."

LouAnn got up from her rocking chair with great effort. She shuffled into the kitchen. Came back out with a dirty tray carrying hockey-puck-sized cookies.

"I am not used to gettin' company in these parts, forgive me. You want one?" Before they could answer, she was handing Maddy and Owen each one.

"Thank you," Owen replied. He took a bite of his cookie. It tasted a little like ketchup. Still he smiled. He gave LouAnn a silent thumbs up as he choked down the bite.

She plopped back in her chair again. "We seen your mom just last night. Boy! You sure do look like her. Your brown hair and dimples. You are the spitting image of her. Real beauty. Now, I don't know how she knowed to come here, but she was looking for something."

Merl said, "See, now, people come round here thinking they know the river. Thinkin' it is just some water flowin' to the Gulf of Mexico. For centuries people have gathered at the river. A lot of blood has been shed at this river. Truth is, the river is full of spirits—some good, some not. And some spirits find homes in its caves."

LouAnn cut him off. "I can read people, you know, see their souls. I knew she could be trusted. We lent her the atlas."

Maddy remembered the book that was sticking out of her mom's bag the last time she saw her mom.

"It was an atlas my great-grandpa got from a flea market. It had what your mom was lookin' for. LouAnn, she a real good judge of character. She said your ma could be trusted, so we lent her the atlas. She said we'd be savin' lives. I know she's right. Your ma is a real straight shooter. You find the atlas, you'll find your mom."

"Do you know where we might look for the atlas?" Maddy asked.

"Well, your mom, she talked about the island just three miles down the river from here. It's called Pig's Eye Island."

"Pig's Eye Island?" asked Owen.

Merl glared at LouAnn. "It's a place you shouldn't be asking about. You'd be best to forget you ever heard of a place called that."

"Evil visits there. It don't live there; nothing can live there. But still, it ain't no place for young folks," explained LouAnn.

"We have to get going," Maddy said abruptly. She stood up to leave.

Merl shook his head. "I wouldn't advise you go to Pig's Eye Island, but if you are stupid enough to, be sure to go only when the sun shines. And the island can flood in minutes. You got to watch the shore. Always watch the shore."

He propped the door open for Maddy and Owen. The snakes were once again in full view, slithering and wiggling in the grass. Maddy gave a little yelp.

LouAnn explained, "This area used to be part of the river. It seems that the snakes don't know that it ain't a river no more. They are harmless, darlin'."

Maddy tried not to show how much she didn't like snakes. Owen and Maddy thanked the couple and walked to the car.

Then LouAnn hollered from the doorway, "Your heart will lead you to your mom. Don't believe what you see. Eyes deceive, but your heart won't!"

Maddy waved once she got in the car. She checked her cell phone for a message, text or voice, from her mom.

Nothing.

Owen saw the disappointment on Maddy's face. "Well, are we going to need the canoe?"

CHAPTER 7

"We have to go to Pig's Eye Island," Maddy stated matter-of-factly.

"I thought you would say that," replied Owen. They were almost home by now. "We should probably wait until tomorrow, though. It's getting kind of late. You heard what the swamp people said. By the time we get the canoe, strap it to the roof of the car, and get to the landing, let alone paddle to the island, we will barely have enough time to look around."

"No way. It could be too late." Maddy gave him a determined look, then a kiss.

"Then I guess we'd better hurry," he said.

He knew there was no way she was going to take no for an answer. They held hands the rest of the way home, like an old married couple. They got to his house and packed the canoe, paddles, and life jackets.

Finally they were off to the boat landing, where they parked the car. Maddy and Owen carefully slid the wooden canoe off of the roof of the car. They hauled it to the water. Owen held the canoe as Maddy tried to keep her balance getting into the tippy boat.

There was a gentle breeze. It was too early in the season for mosquitoes. It would have been the perfect day for a canoe trip, but instead there was a hurry to everything. Time felt very precious. Owen and Maddy rowed in sync with each other. Their paddles dipped into the water, pushing and lifting at exactly the same time. They moved quickly and smoothly upstream. Maddy's arms ached. Her injured hands burned. They spotted the muddy banks of Pig's Eye Island. It was covered in dead trees that had no leaves, or even bark. During floods the water drowned the trees and pulled off all the bark.

They dragged the canoe up onto the shore of the island.

It was silent. There was nothing living on the island except the crows. They cawed from the bare branches. Maddy started to walk around the very small piece of land. There were clouds of gnats buzzing around them.

The sun was getting low in the sky. "Let's split up," said Maddy. "We need to cover this island quickly."

Owen continued to walk around the edge of the island. Maddy walked toward its center. She came to a clearing where there were no trees. There was a smooth floor of wet clay, a greasy mud that covered the island. Maddy walked through it. At first, she left perfect shoe prints. She could see every zigzag and line on the bottom of her shoes imprinted into the clay. But as Maddy kept walking, clay gathered on the bottom of her shoes. Every step became a little heavier. She kept walking even though the heels of her shoes were starting to slip under the weight of the clay.

Then she saw a footprint, not her own, perfectly imprinted into the clay. It had a unique pattern and looked about the same size as Maddy's. She squatted down to get a closer look at the pattern. She saw the Zoot logo. That was the brand name of her mom's running shoes. These were definitely her mom's shoe prints. Maddy followed them. She walked about twenty feet. The prints came to an end. There were no other tracks. The river was still another twenty feet away. There was nowhere for Mom to go, and yet the prints stopped. It was like she had just vanished.

Maddy heard her name. It was Owen.

"Maddy! We have to go!" shouted Owen. "The island is flooding."

"Look at this. Mom was here!"

"Come on, Maddy! We have to get to the canoe before it floats away."

Maddy tried to run to him, but her feet were stuck. The clay had formed a cement around her shoes. She quickly untied her laces. She stepped out of her shoes and ran to the shore barefoot. The water had reached the canoe. She was about to climb in when she looked up in a tree. She saw something red. Maddy jumped out of the canoe. She ran to the tree.

There, wedged between a cluster of branches, was the atlas. She used smaller branches that were low to the ground to help her climb. Already the ground she had run on was covered in cold river water flooding the island. She grabbed the book, but there was no way down.

Owen paddled around the trees that were getting covered by more water. He fought the current, trying with all of his strength to steady the canoe under Maddy so she could jump in.

"Climb down as far as you can and then jump," said Owen.

"I'm going to tip the canoe."

"It's the only option we have right now. The sun's setting. We have to get out of here! Come on, Maddy. Jump!"

Owen held onto both sides of the canoe. He spread his weight out so the canoe would be steadier. Maddy jumped. The current spun them around and Owen had to grab the paddles to keep from being tipped over.

"We did it!" Maddy reached over to hug Owen. One side of the canoe dipped into the river.

"Whoa, Maddy! You can thank me when we're home and dry!"

The journey back home was easier. They paddled with the current. Maddy kept thinking about her mom's footprints. Where did they disappear to? More importantly, had her *mom* disappeared? Maddy looked down at the atlas resting on her lap. *The Atlas of Cursed Places*, it read.

"Where are you, Mom?" Maddy whispered.

CHAPTER 8

Maddy and Owen were soaked, cold, and exhausted. Once they had cleaned up and put on warm clothes, they sat down at Maddy's kitchen table.

"Those were my mom's footprints. I just wish I knew where she went. The footprints stopped. It was like she just disappeared."

"Didn't LouAnn say that if we found the atlas, we'd find your mom? Well, here it is." Owen held up *The Atlas of Cursed Places*. "Now where's your mom?"

"That's what I'm afraid of," Maddy said. "Plus, it's not like her to treat someone's stuff so carelessly."

"Maybe she wasn't being careless," said Owen. "I mean, she did have to climb the tree and tuck it among those branches so it wouldn't fall. It isn't like she dropped it in the mud."

"Why would she do that?" asked Maddy. "Unless she had to get rid of it fast. Maybe someone was after her. Then we would have found another set of footprints, right? What dangerous thing could be after my mom but leave no footprints?"

"I don't know, Maddy," replied Owen. "Maybe this will have some answers," he said, pointing at *The Atlas of Cursed Places*.

Maddy carefully opened the old book. On the first page was a map, and scattered throughout the map were skulls. Suddenly, the pages began flipping themselves! Just as suddenly, they stopped.

Maddy and Owen looked at the page. It was the beginning of an entry titled "The Curse of Pike's Cave."

Maddy read out loud to Owen:

Pike's Cave has existed since evil began. Just fifty paces downriver from Minnehaha Falls, this cave was carved by the angry force of the Mississippi River. Some places on Earth have healing powers for good; Pike's Cave is the opposite. It enslaves people and steals their lives. Why it exists is unclear. Perhaps to balance out the powers of good in the world, or create chaos where there is too much order.

WARNING: DO NOT VISIT THIS CAVE. YOU WOULD BE BETTER OFF DROWNING ON YOUR WAY THERE.

"Is that your mom's handwriting?" Owen pointed to a number that had been written on the corner of the atlas's page. "Looks like a phone number."

Maddy took out her phone and dialed the ten digits. The phone rang three times. A woman with a raspy voice picked up.

"Hi there, sugar! Whatcha ya got shakin'?" the woman said.

Maddy didn't know what to say. She was afraid that if she said too much, the woman might hang up, but if Maddy said nothing, the woman would hang up for sure. "Hi, this is Maddy Connelly."

"Maddy. I know your mom," said the woman.

"How do you know her?" asked Maddy.

"How about we meet in person. I can explain everything then," replied the friendly woman. "Could we meet tomorrow afternoon?"

Maddy wanted to meet right that very second. She wasn't sure she could stand to wait until the next afternoon. But she managed to restrain herself

"That'd be okay. How about Grounds Coffee and Pastry?"

"Peachy. See you there about three."

Maddy replied, "Okay. Um, I know this is strange to ask, but who are you?"

"Oh, I'm Willow."

Maddy waited for her to elaborate, but she didn't.

"See you soon, sugar," the woman said.

Then she hung up.

CHAPTER 9

Whiny music blared on the speakers. The roasting coffee beans smelled more like burnt toast than coffee. Maddy stood at the counter waiting for the barista to notice her. Finally Maddy fake-coughed. The woman, wearing all black, including her lipstick, walked slowly to Maddy. The barista said nothing. She just waited for Maddy to speak.

"I would like a peppermint mocha," said Maddy.

The barista rolled her eyes at Maddy like she had just been asked to make a steaming cup of dog doo. Then she turned and walked away.

A woman wearing a long skirt, flowy scarf, and gold hoop earrings walked up and stood next to Maddy. She stared at Maddy until Maddy could feel her eyes.

Maddy turned and asked the strange woman, "What do you want?"

"You sure are Eleanor's daughter," said the woman. Her smile was jolly and warm. "I'd know that snarl anywhere."

Then she let out a loud laugh, holding her tummy. Everyone in the coffee shop turned and glared. This was the kind of place where laughing was not in style. The barista handed Maddy the cup. The strange woman stepped in front of Maddy and paid. Then she turned to Maddy and said, "I'm Willow. You must be Maddy?"

They weaved their way to the back of the coffee shop, where there was a booth. Willow sat across from Maddy.

"You look just like your mother."

"How do you know my mom?"

Willow shifted in her chair. "Well, I work with your mom on many of her cases."

"So you work for the St. Paul Police Department?"

"Not exactly. More of a consultant."

Maddy looked really confused.

"I am a psychic. Your mom comes to me for advice."

"On cases?" Maddy was totally shocked. Her mom actually believed in psychics and ghosts and stuff? "You actually help her solve cases?"

"Lots of them," Willow said. "Your mom has seen enough to know that you can't always trust what you see. She and I get together for coffee every week. She has grown to be a dear friend."

Maddy started to get uncomfortable. "I know this is going to sound crazy, but I was at this restaurant built in a cave. See, I met a woman. She wasn't really there, but I could have sworn she was. I think she was a ghost."

Maddy waited for Willow to laugh. Instead Willow waited for Maddy to continue. She was taking every word seriously.

When Maddy didn't keep talking, Willow said, "Yeah, I bet that was Betty. She had really pale skin, wore a gray dress?"

Maddy felt like hugging Willow. "Yes! That was her! We were talking, and all of a sudden the ceiling collapsed on her. Just before all of the rocks fell on her, she said 'It was Pike.' My mom, in my dream, said the same thing. Even Sergeant Riley mentioned the word *Pike* when he was talking about the case my mom is solving right now. Who is this Pike?"

Willow got a very concerned look on her face. She said, "Well, Betty knows Pike well. She knows how he ruins lives. This is going to be very hard to believe. Please have an open mind." She spoke very carefully. "Pike can jump into another person and make their body do whatever he wants. Kind of like driving a car. He just hops in and does all the steering." She leaned into the table to be closer to Maddy. "Poor Betty shot up that restaurant you saw her in. That was about eighty years ago. She said it was Pike. Of course, you can't put an evil spirit on trial for murder. She took all the blame. After all, it was her hands doing all of the killing. She killed herself before the trial started. The strange thing is, she told me that while the massacre was happening, she could still think and feel; she just had no control over her body." Willow was all choked up. "Such a sweet soul, isn't she? Sometimes I go and have lunch with her. You should see the waiters look when I start talking to her. They think I'm crazy."

"What happened to Pike?" Maddy was getting uneasy.

"Well, shortly after the massacre and suicide, the SPPD sealed up the cave. Pike hasn't been seen since."

Color drained from Maddy's face. Her eyes dropped to the table.

"What happened?" Willow lifted Maddy's chin. Looking hard into Maddy's eyes, she said, "How much trouble is she in?"

Maddy didn't want to cry in front of Willow. "I haven't seen my mom in almost two days. She's missing. I guess the police department is still able to track her squad car. They say she is moving around the city. They say she is just really into this case. But, Willow, I always hear from my mom, *always*! But I haven't heard a thing since early Sunday morning."

"And that's why you called me."

"I found your number in *The Atlas of Cursed Places*. My mom wrote it in there."

"LouAnn and Merl lent it to your mom?" asked Willow.

"They did. But my boyfriend and I—"

"Owen."

"How'd you know that? Psychic powers?"

Willow laughed. "Your mom told me."

"Oh. Right. Anyway, yeah, Owen and I went to Pig's Eye Island because LouAnn said my mom was heading there. She said that if we found the atlas, we'd find my mom. We went there and found the atlas in a tree, but no Mom. Only her footprints that seemed to vanish into thin air."

Willow was sensing more than Maddy was saying. She could feel Maddy's fear. She could feel something else. Something cold and empty. Willow said, "You must have just missed her on the island. Let me see what I can do. Do you have anything of your mom's?"

"Just the atlas with her handwriting," replied Maddy.

"Perfect. Open it up." Willow hovered her hand over the numbers Maddy's mom had written. "Give me your hand."

Willow closed her eyes and went into a trance. At first she gently swayed from side to side. Maddy looked around, hoping no one in the coffee shop would notice. Willow's eyes fluttered. She pushed her hand against the numbers in the atlas and squeezed Maddy's hand. Maddy wanted to yelp in pain. Willow started to rock violently. Her grip on Maddy tightened. The pain was so bad that Maddy wanted to break free from Willow's hand but couldn't. The table shook. People were starting to point and whisper. Willow mumbled something that didn't sound like English. Maddy didn't know what to do. She was about to yell for help when Willow's eyes popped open. They were filled with tears.

"Pike is back." Her voice quivered in fear as she spoke. Silent tears started to run down her cheeks.

"Please, Willow. Where is Mom? She's all I've got."

Willow snapped out of her stare. "I am sorry, sweetie. It is bad, really bad."

"What is it? Does it have something to do with this cave?" Maddy pointed to the cave in the atlas.

"No. It has *everything* to do with the cave. You see, the cave is like a vacuum. It sucks the living into its darkness. I am afraid your mom is heading right for it. The case is leading her there."

"We have to destroy the cave!" Maddy yelled. People in the coffee shop were glaring at them.

"Evil takes many forms. Like energy, it can never die; it simply changes form. If you destroy the cave, who knows what form it will take."

"Are we still talking about Pike?" Maddy asked.

Willow bent near to Maddy. "The evil that we call Pike can only live in the cave, but if a human is able to enter the cave, Pike can take hold of that person's body and walk out of the cave and do terrible things. Pike is after her."

"But I thought all evil was sealed in the cave!" Maddy said, wishing it to be true.

"It is, but if the seal is broken, people can get in. If someone enters Pike's Cave, he can take over their body and make them do terrible things, like murder a whole room of people."

"So Pike, this evil spirit, can't leave the cave unless he has somebody else's body?" asked Maddy.

"Correct. The only way he can get out is if he possesses someone else's body. Then he just walks right out and works his evil through that person's body."

"Maybe the missing couple found a way into the cave," said Maddy.

"You are a natural-born detective like your mom." Willow gulped loud enough for Maddy to hear.

"She is a good detective. She will find that couple. And if they are in the cave, she will go inside that cave. Is there anyone who has ever made it out without Pike possessing them?"

Willow could tell Maddy was planning something. "Listen to me. If you go in there, you probably will make it out, but Pike will also leave with you. He will make your body do terrible, murderous things around the city. All you will be able to do is watch. You will have no control over the blood that is shed by your hands. You do not want to be responsible for that kind of evil escaping."

"Willow." Maddy had a determined look in her eyes. "Is there any chance that I could escape from the cave with my mom, and only my mom?"

Willow shuddered and with an exasperated exhale said, "There is a chance, yes. But a very small one. For your sake and the people around you, I hope you don't take that chance." Willow took one last sip of coffee. Then she stood up and hugged Maddy. "I have to be going. Betty and I are meeting for dinner.

"Betty! She's okay?"

"Of course she is. You can't get deader than dead." Willow turned and walked out.

Maddy picked up her cell phone and texted Owen to get the canoe ready.

CHAPTER 10

Maddy hopped into Owen's car. He had the canoe strapped to the top of it.

Maddy's eyes were narrow and focused. She could feel the space between her eyebrows wrinkle just like her mom's. She didn't say anything when she got in.

"So do you mind telling me your plan?" asked Owen. "Last I read, we were to stay away from Pike's Cave."

"Plans change, Owen," Maddy said. "We're just going to check out the river. See if we come across anything suspicious. I just want to scope it out. I promise I won't do anything stupid; I just want to see what the cave looks like. From the outside, of course."

"We only have about two hours of daylight. We don't want to get stuck on the river when it gets dark."

They drove to Minnehaha Falls. Then they hiked a little downstream. Owen found a clearing. They carefully slid the canoe into the river.

As they paddled, Maddy noticed how quiet the evening was. Usually there were frogs, birds, even the occasional muskrat. But this evening . . . nothing. The current had even slowed down. The wind held its breath. The only sound was a distant thumping noise. It got louder as they paddled on. It didn't sound as though it came from nature. More metallic. Like metal hitting rock.

Maddy's heart raced. Her palms were sweaty. She could feel a darkness getting closer and closer. It was made up of a deep loneliness and a deeper fear.

"You want to turn back?" asked Owen. He was nervous. The current sped up. Large boulders stuck out of the water. Owen barely steered the canoe around one of them. The river narrowed. The thumping became a loud clanging.

"Maddy! I'm turning back."

"No! Let's make it around this curve. We can turn back then." Maddy could feel something pulling her further down the river.

As they came around the curve, there was something large bobbing in the water. It was shiny and white. Maddy pointed to the object. Owen steered the canoe toward what looked like a sunken boat. They were almost on top of it. It wasn't a boat at all. It was a squad car. *Floating in the river.* It had been caught on a boulder. Maddy leaned over, almost tipping the canoe.

"Oh, my God! It's my mom's squad. She is number 719."

Owen could hardly keep her in the canoe while he called the police from his cell. When she managed to jump into the river, she didn't even notice the freezing water. The ice had melted off only a few weeks ago. She clung to the white metal of her mom's squad car, trying desperately to look inside. She clumsily swam around to each window and peered in. Nothing. No one. No sign her mom was ever there. Maddy felt relief. She swam to the front of the car, resisting the strong river current. She climbed on top of the hood of the car, thinking she could lie there for a brief rest.

When she reached the glass, she saw the words "Save Me" scratched into the windshield. The letters were written backwards because they had been written from the inside of the car. Maddy went limp. Her body slid down the hood of the floating car and into the cold river water.

"Maddy! Maddy!" Owen pushed the paddle as fast as he could through the water. He caught up to her. The canoe was too tippy to pull her on board. He jumped out of the canoe, flipping it over, and pushed Maddy on top of the upside-down boat. He swam them to the shore.

On shore he pulled Maddy close to him to keep her warm. She was alive but limp.

Her lips were blue. She shook uncontrollably. The sun was down by this time. Owen heard footsteps getting closer. Flashlights darted around until one of the beams of light landed on Owen's face. A police officer was holding the flashlight, and Owen could make out several other officers in the dark, also holding flashlights. Maddy was breathing, but her color was gray. Owen lifted her.

"She needs help," Owen shouted.

He carried her to the safety of a dry, waiting squad car. An officer wrapped her in a wool blanket and drove her and Owen back to the station. By the time they arrived, the color had returned to Maddy's face. She was sitting up, watching out the window. She still didn't talk.

The police officer looked in the rearview mirror and said, "The sergeant wants to have a few words with you."

CHAPTER 11

They waited late into the night. Finally, Sergeant Riley walked into the station. He had dark circles under his eyes. He had clearly not shaved for several days. He walked up to Maddy.

"Do you know where my mom is?" Maddy could see in Sargeant Riley's eyes that something was off.

"Come in, Maddy," Sergeant Riley said. Then he extended a hand to Owen. "Hello there. Sergeant Mark Riley. A friend and coworker of Eleanor Connelly, Maddy's mom."

"Nice to meet you," Owen said.

"Have a seat," said the sergeant, motioning to a couple of chairs in his office. "Would you like anything to drink? Water, coffee . . . well, I guess just water or coffee."

"No," said Maddy.

There was a long pause while Sergeant Riley sat down behind his large desk piled with papers.

"I'm not going to be telling you anything new, Maddy. Your mom is missing. That is her car that we pulled out of the river. The good news is that there was no trace of your mom or any foul play. In fact, there are no clues at all, really."

"Except for the words 'Save Me' scratched into the glass of the windshield. I would call that a really big clue!"

Sergeant Riley looked like he was about to cry. "Listen, Maddy. Your mom is like a little sister to me. I will not stop until I find her."

"What about the cave? Did you check there?" asked Maddy.

"Cave?" asked Sergeant Riley.

"Come on, Sergeant, you know about the cave! Just because it's sealed off doesn't mean it doesn't exist!"

"Listen, Maddy. I am doing the best I can to get your mom back, but you need to calm down. You aren't helping matters."

"But there is this cave where evil lives. The missing couple's probably there. My mom's going to find the couple, which means she is going to be heading right for the cave."

"Maddy, I think you need to leave the detective work to us. That's a little far-fetched. If you hear from your mom, please call immediately."

"But how? You can't even keep track of a freaking squad car, let alone a human." Maddy could feel the lump in her throat. "And that human is the only family I have."

Maddy stood up and walked out of his office, slamming the door so hard it rattled pictures on the walls. When Maddy reached Owen's car, she turned to him and said, "It's up to us now. Are you in?"

"I'm all in."

CHAPTER 12

"We need to make a plan, Maddy,"
Owen said as they drove back to Maddy's
house. "We keep talking about this cave.
Everything seems to point to this cave. We
have to find it!"

"What if everything people say about the
cave is true?" asked Maddy.

"Maddy, I can't believe I'm saying this—
we're talking about risking our lives—but you
will never forgive yourself if you don't at least
try. Besides, if anyone can overcome an evil,
life-eating demon, it's you."

Maddy smiled and gave Owen a huge hug.
The car swerved into the other lane.

"Easy, we still need to live through this ride home."

Owen pulled over and parked when he got to Maddy's house. She kissed him passionately. It felt so good to be in his arms and feel his lips on hers.

Maddy slid out of the car and turned around. "Well, are you coming?"

"I just thought—" Owen was not used to being invited into her house this late at night.

"We need to make a plan if we're going to find my mom tomorrow."

"Very true," Owen said.

They sat at the kitchen table Googling images of the river, pinpointing where they had found her mom's squad car and where the cave might be.

"So once we find this cave, then what?" asked Owen.

"Then I don't know. I go in?" Maddy replied.

"*We* go in," Owen corrected Maddy.

"You're not going to follow me in there. Besides, someone has to stay outside in case we need to call the police."

"Maddy, you don't get to decide for me. Now, what will we need to bust open a sealed cave and defeat an evil spirit?" Owen typed it into Google.

Maddy held her hands up. "I don't know, peanut butter and jelly?"

It felt good to laugh. Even if it wasn't that funny. Things had been so serious and they had felt so powerless. But now, finally they had a plan.

The sun was almost up by the time Owen left. They decided they would get a few hours of sleep and leave after lunch. Maddy lay her head on the pillow. For the first time in what felt like forever, she fell asleep before her restless mind started to worry.

But even in Maddy's sleep she couldn't escape Pike. He was there. She could hear him breathing just behind her ear. Maddy's eyes popped open. The breathing must have been a dream, but she couldn't shake the feeling that someone was in the house.

It was almost noon. Owen would be there soon. She got into the shower, hoping to lose the icky feeling. She let the hot water run down her back. She was sore from last night's swim in the cold river. The words "Save Me" echoed in her head. She stepped out of the shower and began to towel off.

Then, just as she lifted her head to look in the mirror, she saw a figure standing just behind her left shoulder. It was the shadow of a person. Maddy spun around. She saw no one. And then, as if spoken into her ear, a low demonic voice whispered, "It is me." Then Maddy was alone. She could feel that she was alone.

She quickly got dressed, putting on layers because she had read that caves were very cold. She had a flashlight and her cell phone in case she ran into trouble. She sat down to eat a peanut butter and jelly sandwich, but just then Owen pulled up and gave a quick beep. Just as she was about to leave, she spotted her mom's pocketknife and slipped it into her pocket.

Owen beeped again. She ran to the car, her sandwich hanging out of her mouth.

"Breakfast of champions, huh?"

With a huge bite in her mouth she replied, "You know it." She swallowed and then gave him a peanut buttery kiss.

"How'd you sleep?" asked Owen.

"Like the dead," replied Maddy.

CHAPTER 13

They reached Minnehaha Falls. Police
tape blocked off where they had previously
entered the water. Owen retrieved the
canoe from the roof of the car. Maddy
ripped the police tape down. They
wouldn't be needing that. They hiked
toward the river. The riverbank was steep
and slippery with wet mud. Owen led the
way down it. A large black crow cawed
from a distance.

"It seems more difficult to get to the river
today than it was the first time," Owen said.

Maddy felt the same way, but didn't let on.
"We're just more tired, that's all."

Owen took small, careful steps, but even then his heel slipped and he lost his balance. He fell in the cold, wet mud. Maddy lost her grip on the canoe. Owen and the canoe slid to the river's edge.

"Are you okay?" She ran to the water.

"Yeah." He was holding his shoulder.

They finally made it to the water and began to paddle downstream. As they paddled, Maddy noticed a crow following them. Watching them. Dark, heavy clouds moved in, blocking out the sun.

Owen looked up at the sky. "A little rain can't stop us."

They kept paddling, watching the riverbank.

"This is where Mom's squad car was found," Maddy said. "Keep your eyes open for what looks like an entrance to a cave."

They had to weave around more large boulders.

"I had no idea there were so many animals here!" Maddy pointed out. "I swear I just saw like three deer running that way." She was pointing upstream, the opposite direction from where they were heading.

"I know! I just saw a fox running the same direction."

Then they saw more deer, raccoons, rabbits, even coyotes, all running the opposite direction they were heading.

"Maddy! Look!" Owen pointed to two large brown bears running at full speed. "What are they all running towards?"

Maddy didn't say anything. Fear grew inside her like a cancer. She looked up into the trees. "Or maybe they're running *from* something."

Owen's paddle stopped. It was one thing to talk about spirits and evil beings, but it was another thing to actually witness it. He took a deep breath and dipped his paddle once more in the water.

Pulling the blade of their paddles through the water was becoming increasingly difficult.

The crow that had been following them since they arrived flew low and landed on the front of the boat. Its black, beady eyes stared at Maddy, and it let out three loud caws, as if to tell them to turn back. Owen shooed it off the boat. The crow swooped low and nipped at Owen's head.

"Ow! I think he actually got a clump of my hair," Owen said, holding his head.

Maddy pulled his head to her lips and kissed where the crow had attacked him. "There, all better." She smiled.

It fell completely silent around them. No wind to rustle the trees. No birds singing. No insects buzzing. The river had slowed to a standstill.

"That's strange," Owen said. "We're circling around like a whirlpool."

"Or a tornado. Look up there." Maddy pointed to the sky. The clouds rotated in a circle as silent bolts of lightning zapped the earth.

Owen wasn't looking at the sky. He was speechless. He grabbed Maddy's arm and pulled her so she would look at the giant cement wall fixed onto the side of the riverbank.

"Holy crap!" Maddy said. "I think that's what we've been looking for. They used cement to seal off the main entrance of the cave."

The cement wall was covered in graffiti. Maddy and Owen canoed over to the side of the wall.

"Do you hear that?" asked Owen. "It sounds like water dripping."

They pulled the canoe onto the rocky riverbank. Walking was difficult because the riverbank had changed from slippery mud to sandstone that crumbled beneath their feet.

"I think it's coming from over here," said Owen.

They were almost in the river when they found a pile of rocks that looked as if they had come from a different planet. They appeared to be shiny black shards of glass, except thicker and a lot heavier.

"It is! There's water running into these rocks," Maddy yelled excitedly. She could almost feel her mom. They were so close now.

She began to quickly pull the rocks from the pile to see where the water was running.

Owen came over to her just as one of the sharp rocks sliced her finger. Owen glanced at the bloody finger. His face turned white. Maddy quickly put her finger in her pocket. The last thing she needed was to have Owen faint at the sight of her blood.

"There, no blood," Maddy said.

Color returned to his face. Maddy continued to remove the strange black rocks until finally a small opening appeared.

CHAPTER 14

The clouds were so thick in the sky that it seemed like night. The silent lightning was getting closer.

Maddy thought back to her dream. "Stay here," Maddy commanded. "This isn't your fight."

"No, we already talked about this," said Owen. "I go with you. This is my fight too. This Pike thing messes with you, he messes with me."

"Ladies first," Maddy said. She lay down and carefully scooted into the cave on her belly. She could feel the jagged rocks scratch the delicate skin on her stomach. When she stood up, she was in Pike's Cave. She had never seen such blackness. There was absolutely no light.

She didn't realize Owen had joined her until he flipped on his headlamp. "Wow," he whispered. "This is amazing." They were standing on the edge of a huge room made out of stone. It had a thirty-foot ceiling with spikes that looked like rock icicles. Water pooled on the floor. The dripping sound that had led them to the opening was actually the echo of water droplets falling off these rock icicles, or stalactites. She turned on her flashlight. Already she could feel Pike watching them.

There was only one way to go, and that was forward. They walked through the open space, into the unknown darkness. It smelled like dirt and something rotting. Soon the cave narrowed. Owen had to hunch. Maddy's flashlight darted. She was looking for a clue— something that would lead them to her mom. Her focus was so complete, she didn't notice her foot snag something. She crashed to the cold ground. Owen shined his light.

"It's a duffel bag," Owen said. He bent down to free her foot.

"Let me see." Maddy took the bag and opened it. Inside was a jar of peanut butter and jelly and her mom's police badge.

Maddy hadn't felt this excited for days. They walked on. The cave opened a little, so Owen could stand up straight. He paused to stretch and take a look around. Small holes had apparently been drilled into the wall of the cave. He shined his light on more of the rock wall. There were chains attached to it. Maddy tugged on his shirt.

There, stuck to the wall, were two dead bodies. Their skin was thin, pulled tight over their bones. Their lips had rotted away so their white teeth stood out. One body was clearly a woman, the other a man. Neither had shoes.

"The missing couple," Maddy said.

She reached out and grabbed the purse lying next to the dead woman. Then she took a deep breath. Trying hard not to tremble, she lifted the man's overcoat away from his hollow, empty chest. With the very tips of her fingers,

Maddy reached into the inside pocket of the coat. She pulled out his wallet. As she did, her hand brushed the dead man's arm. It was enough force to make his hand fall off his body onto the cold ground next to Maddy's foot. She screamed. Stepped back. She was really more startled than scared of the dead bodies. After all, a dead person can't hurt you.

After the initial shock, she said, "My mom will be happy to see these."

Maddy stuffed the man's wallet into the dead woman's purse. She wrapped the purse across her body.

"Let's just take a moment to honor the dead," said Maddy.

They stood in this evil place saying their own version of a prayer.

Maddy could feel something soft moving over her feet. It was so light she almost didn't feel it. She shook her foot. Then it was back. She shook her foot again, but this time it wrapped around her ankle and wound up her calf. She shined the light on her leg. A snake. No, *snakes*—plural. Maddy kicked her legs and whipped her arms. She bent down and yanked the snakes from her thigh. Involuntarily, she started to run. The slimy creatures wriggled beneath her feet, but she didn't stop. Owen tried to keep up, but in the dark it was difficult. For a long time he just followed the beam of light coming from her flashlight, but soon that disappeared.

He slowed to a walk. He listened in the cave for her voice, her cough, even for her breath, but he heard nothing. Only silence. The narrow cave split into two different passageways. Owen had to make a decision. The left passage was pitch-black. He looked down the right passage and couldn't believe his eyes. There was a dim light at the end of it.

After what Maddy had just gone through, he was certain she had taken the passage to the right, the one with the light at the end. He turned and began his journey toward the orange glow.

CHAPTER 15

Maddy stumbled and tripped over loose rocks. She fell and twisted her ankle. Huddled on the ground, Maddy was surrounded by darkness. The cave smelled like the earth, not rotting flesh and snakes. It was also much colder than before. There was an eerie quiet. Maddy could see her breath in the beam of her flashlight. She trembled. She couldn't tell if it was because she was scared or if it was the cold.

Out of the darkness arms wrapped around her. One around her chest and the other around her mouth.

"Mouse." It was a faint whisper, but it was enough.

"Mom!"

Immediately, Maddy was shushed. "He's out there. The one that killed the couple. The one that is trying to take me. He's looking for me now. I got away, but he will find me and do something awful."

"I'll get us out," Maddy said confidently.

Maddy's mom hugged Maddy tightly and kissed the top of her head. Maddy started to backtrack with her mom close behind her. They got to the split in the cave. Maddy noticed the dim orange light. Her mom adamantly pushed her forward.

Mom whispered, "That is where *he* is. The glow isn't real."

They pushed forward. Past the place where the snakes had been. Past the dead bodies. And finally into the large entrance of the cave. There waited Owen.

Maddy lurched in his direction. She had been so worried. Her mom grabbed her by the shirt.

"Run, Maddy!"

"Mom, it's Owen." Maddy was trying to

free herself from her mom's grasp. "He came here to save you just like I did."

"Look at his eyes, Maddy."

Indeed, there was something intense, something malicious, in those eyes. And yet there was something else, too.

Tears.

Owen was crying.

"Pike is in his body but not his mind," Maddy said, repeating something she'd read in *The Atlas of Cursed Places* and heard from Willow.

Suddenly Owen lunged at Maddy's mom with a rock as sharp as a spear. She dodged him but slipped on some loose gravel. Owen spun around and pinned her to the ground with his boot. He held the stone spike just above her heart, but Maddy grabbed him from behind. She pulled on his neck and beat on his back.

Owen turned. Maddy saw his eyes once more. Tears continued trickling down his face.

He was mortified at what his hands were doing, but he couldn't stop them. They went up to Maddy's throat. They squeezed. Maddy put her hand in her pocket and fumbled around. She found the pocketknife and pulled it out.

"Owen, I am saving you!" Maddy shouted.

She took the knife and pressed the sharp blade into the palm of her hand. Warm blood gushed out. Owen saw the dark, red liquid. His face turned white. His knees quivered, and he fell to the ground. Maddy wrapped a jacket around her hand to stop the bleeding.

Dropping to the cold ground beside Owen, she brushed the hair from his eyes and gently kissed him. His eyes fluttered open.

"I love you, Owen. I always have," Maddy said with tears pouring down her cheeks. He gave her a wide grin.

"We have to leave, now! Pike will come back and use one of us," Mom commanded.

"Owen, you have to get up. Can you do that for me?"

Owen nodded, still groggy from fainting.

They slid out of the small opening. First Owen, then Mom, and then Maddy.

The clouds broke apart in the sun. They heard birds in the distance. Owen steadied the canoe as Maddy and her mom stepped into it.

They paddled for a while in silence, catching their breaths.

"So, Detective Connelly?" Owen finally said.

"Yes?" Maddy's mom replied.

"Sorry for trying to, you know, stab you with a rock back there."

"No worries," she said. "Thanks for, you know, coming to my rescue."

"No worries," Owen repeated.

The three of them paddled in silence again.

This time it was Maddy's mom who spoke up. "When we get to shore, how about the three of us grab some dinner?"

"I'd like that," said Owen.

"PB&J?" asked Maddy.

Maddy's mom smiled. "You read my mind."